Archie was a very
BUSY rhino.

His space-station model was bigger
than Mum. And bigger than Dad.
But still NOT big ENOUGH!

MORE!

Tracey Corderoy

Tim Warnes

LITTLE TIGER PRESS
London

Archie was a very HUNGRY rhino too.

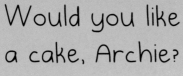

And Archie was a very NOISY rhino.

But even at quiet times, he ALWAYS wanted more . . .

Whatever Archie liked,
he liked it
a LOT.

And whatever Archie did, he always did that *little* bit extra . . .

Archie's costume was AMAZING. Everyone thought so . . .

But it did make Archie too **slow**
to catch up . . .

too **heavy** to bounce . . .

Maybe "more" WASN'T
always more fun.

Maybe "more" was sometimes
TOO MUCH . . .

wheeeee!

Except, of course . . .

. . . when it came to having more

FRIENDS!